KIRSTEN'S PROMISE

KIRSTEN · 1854

BY JANET SHAW

ILLUSTRATIONS RENÉE GRAEF, KIM LEWIS

VIGNETTES SUSAN MCALILEY

THE AMERICAN GIRLS COLLECTION®

Published by Pleasant Company Publications
Previously published in *American Girl*® magazine
Copyright © 2003 by Pleasant Company
For information, address: Book Editor, Pleasant Company Publications,
8400 Fairway Place, P.O. Box 620998, Middleton, WI 53562.

Visit our Web site at **americangirl.com**

Printed in Singapore.
03 04 05 06 07 08 09 10 TWP 10 9 8 7 6 5 4 3 2 1

The American Girls Collection® and logo, American Girls Short Stories™,
the American Girl logo, Kirsten®, and Kirsten Larson®
are trademarks of Pleasant Company.

Library of Congress Cataloging-in-Publication Data

Shaw, Janet Beeler, 1937–
Kirsten's Promise / by Janet Shaw ; illustrations, Renée Graef, Kim Lewis ;
vignettes, Susan McAliley.
p. cm. — (The American girls collection)
Summary: Ten-year-old Kirsten regrets the promise she has made to a ragged boy
she discovers alone near a wrecked covered wagon not far from her
Minnesota home.

ISBN 1-58485-696-3
[1. Promises—Fiction. 2. Frontier and pioneer life—Minnesota—Fiction. 3. Swedish
Americans—Fiction. 4. Minnesota—History—To 1858—Fiction.] I. Graef, Renée, ill.
II. Lewis, Kim, ill. III. McAliley, Susan, ill. IV. Title. V. Series.
PZ7.S53423 Kit 2003   [Fic]—dc21   2002029672

The
AMERICAN GIRLS
COLLECTION®

PICTURE CREDITS

The following individuals and organizations have generously given permission to reprint illustrations contained in "Looking Back": p. 30—Photo by Bruce Hucko; p. 31—Library of Congress; p. 32—The Church of Jesus Christ of Latter-Day Saints; p. 34—Benjamin Franklin Reinhart, *The Emigrant Train Bedding Down for the Night,* 1867 (detail; see full image below), oil on canvas, 40 x 70 inches, in the collection of The Corcoran Gallery of Art, gift of Mr. and Mrs. Lansdell K. Christie; p. 35—Courtesy Pike's Peak Library District; p. 36—Nebraska State Historical Society (RG3314); p. 37—Sheet music, Duke University, Rare Book, Manuscript & Special Collections Library; p. 38—Library of Congress; p. 39—Receipt book, Barclay & Co., publisher, Courtesy Minnesota Historical Society; Medicine chest, Oregon Historical Society (Or Hi 59049); p. 40—Wyoming State Archives; p. 42—Photography by Jamie Young.

Reinhart's *Emigrant Train,* 1867

TABLE OF CONTENTS

KIRSTEN'S FAMILY

PAPA
Kirsten's father, who is sometimes gruff but always loving.

MAMA
Kirsten's mother, who never loses heart.

KIRSTEN
A ten-year-old who moves with her family to a new home on America's frontier in 1854.

LARS
Kirsten's fifteen-year-old brother, who is almost a man.

PETER
*Kirsten's mischievous
brother, who is
seven years old.*

BRITTA
*Kirsten's baby sister,
who is five months old.*

EZRA
*Kirsten's new friend,
a little boy with a
big secret.*

KIRSTEN'S
PROMISE

"Caro, go home!" Kirsten Larson stamped her foot at her dog, who was following right at her heels. "You can't come to school with me! Now go on home."

Caro paused, his breath making white puffs in the chill October air. But he didn't head back toward the Larsons' little cabin in the Minnesota woods. Instead, he cocked his head, listening to something Kirsten

1

couldn't hear, then dashed off down the wooded hill beside the road, barking excitedly. In a moment, another dog began barking and growling, too. *Oh, no!* Kirsten thought. *A dogfight!*

She ran down the hill after Caro. There, in a clearing, she found him barking at a large black dog with a grizzled muzzle who crouched on a low pile of stones. The dog's ears were laid back and its teeth bared. Nearby, a canvas-topped wagon lay on its side. In front of the wagon stood a small boy Kirsten had never seen before. He wore a jacket buttoned crookedly, and he held a rifle aimed straight at Caro. "Get your dog away from here!" he yelled.

Startled, Kirsten grabbed Caro and

"Get your dog away from here!" he yelled.

pulled him against her legs. The black dog continued to growl, but it didn't leave the pile of stones.

Holding Caro close, Kirsten moved backward, her gaze on the overturned wagon. Boxes and pots and blankets lay strewn on the rocky ground beside a split wagon wheel. A spotted horse grazed on the frosty grass. "It looks like your wheel broke," Kirsten said.

"What if it did?" the boy said gruffly.

The boy wasn't much bigger than Kirsten's little brother, Peter, so she was more curious than scared. "You're not from around here," Kirsten said. "Where are you from?"

The boy scowled but lowered his rifle a bit. "We came from up north."

Kirsten glanced around, but she didn't see anyone except this scruffy boy with tangled hair. "We? Who's with you?"

"My ma's with me, that's who," the boy said. He scowled more darkly.

Behind him, Kirsten noticed now, a woman's clothes spilled out of a smashed trunk. "Has your mama gone to get help?" she asked.

"That's none of your business," he said. "You just go on wherever you're going."

But Kirsten was much too curious to be turned away. "I'm going to school," she said. "Where are you and your mama going?"

"We're going to California," the boy

said. "My pa's out there. We're going to join my pa."

"But you can't travel west in the winter!" Kirsten said. "Snowdrifts will close all the passes through the mountains."

"Well, I know *that!*" he said. "We're going to stay with friends in Red Wing. We'd be there now if the wheel hadn't broken. Come spring, we'll go downriver and join a wagon train. That's all I got to say."

"At least tell me your name," she urged him. "I'll tell you mine. I'm Kirsten Larson."

The boy shrugged. "I'm Ezra. Go on along now."

But Kirsten wanted to help. "Ezra, my papa would be glad to fix your wagon wheel," she said. "Papa can fix about anything! You and your mama can keep warm in our cabin while he works. I'll go get him now!"

Ezra seemed to bristle. "You leave me alone!" He raised the rifle, and the black dog growled loudly in response. "We're not going anywhere! And you're not to tell anyone we're here. You got to promise!" He pointed the rifle at Kirsten. "Promise, or I'll fix you!" he hissed.

Now Kirsten *was* frightened. She didn't understand this rude boy, Ezra. And what did he mean he'd "fix" her if she told anyone she'd seen him? She would let him stay here, if that's what he wanted so badly.

"*Promise!*" Ezra repeated.

7

Surely he wouldn't shoot her—would he? The truth was she didn't know what this angry boy might do. "I promise," Kirsten whispered. Keeping Caro at her side, she fled back up through the woods to the road.

❤

At school, Kirsten thought of nothing but Ezra, and the more she thought, the more anxious she became. For all his threats, he was only a skinny little boy in a raggedy jacket. Where had his mother gone? Why didn't Ezra want Papa to help? And why had Ezra made Kirsten promise not to tell anyone that they were there? "Promise!" he'd commanded, and she had. But the more she thought about it, the more the promise felt like a weight in her chest.

After school, Kirsten went looking for her big brother, Lars. She found him chopping firewood behind the barn. Lars had given her good advice before, and she needed some now.

"Remember the time you carved a little deer as a gift for Mama?" Kirsten asked. "You made me promise not to tell about it."

Lars quit chopping and brushed the hair out of his eyes with his wrist. "That's true," he said. "You kept your promise, and Mama was sure surprised!"

"If someone told you a secret and you

9

promised not to tell, would you ever break your promise?" Kirsten asked.

"Never!" Lars said quickly.

"Not ever?" Kirsten persisted. "Can't you think of a single thing that would make you break it?"

Lars leaned on the axe the way Papa did when he stopped work to think things through. "Well, let's see. Maybe if Peter made me promise not to tell he was doing something really dangerous—"

"Like playing on the cliffs where rattlesnakes nest?" Kirsten suggested.

"Yes, something dangerous like that," Lars agreed. "If he might be hurt or killed because I kept my promise to him—well, I'd *have* to tell. A person's life is more

*Lars leaned on the axe the way Papa did
when he stopped work to think things through.*

important than a promise."

"And has anyone ever asked you to keep that kind of promise?" she asked hopefully.

"No. No one's asked me to make a promise I couldn't keep," Lars said. "I'm always as good as my word. How about you, Kirsten?"

"I guess I'm always as good as my word, too," she said hesitantly.

"I thought so!" Lars said with a smile. "Papa says no one will trust us if we're not." He picked up the axe and went back to his work again.

❤

The next morning Kirsten shut Caro

in the barn before hurrying off along the road toward school. She hoped that Ezra's mama had gotten their wheel fixed and that she and Ezra had gone on to Red Wing. Curious to find out, Kirsten crept down the hill to the clearing.

Everything was just as before. The broken wagon wheel lay in the dust beside the overturned wagon. The horse nosed at the rocky ground for grass. The black dog lay resting on the pile of stones. As she watched, the dog got to its feet, sniffed the cold wind, and began to bark. Ezra scrambled out from under the canvas wagon top, the rifle in his hand. "Who's there?" he called. His eyes were wide and his face pale beneath the dirt.

"It's only me!" Kirsten stepped quickly forward. She wasn't a bit afraid of him now—maybe because he looked so thin and tired, or maybe because he looked so frightened himself. "You don't need the gun, Ezra," she said.

"You again!" Ezra said. With a sigh, he set down the rifle and spat something he'd been chewing onto the ground.

"I wanted to see if you'd gone on your way," Kirsten said. "What's that you're eating?"

"I'm *trying* to eat dried beans," Ezra said. "It's like eating gravel."

Kirsten opened her lunch *tine,* took out a thick slice of bread and some cold pork, and offered the food to Ezra. He took it without hesitation and ate greedily.

Then she held out a scrap of pork fat to the black dog. It sniffed hungrily and whined, but instead of coming for the scrap, it only crouched lower on the pile of stones.

"Here," Ezra said, taking the scrap and bringing it to his dog.

Looking around, Kirsten saw only one bed of blankets beneath the canvas wagon top. The cookstove lay upside down among the empty pots. "Your mama hasn't come back, has she?" Kirsten said.

Still chewing, Ezra turned and glared at her.

For the first time, Kirsten noticed

streaks of white on his dirty cheeks. Had he been crying? "Listen, Ezra, come home with me," Kirsten said. "Stay with us until your mama comes back."

Ezra shook his head. "I won't leave," he said.

"Our cabin's not far," Kirsten insisted. "You can come back often to see if your mama's returned. No one will steal your things."

Ezra clenched his fists. "I *can't* leave. My ma said, '*Don't leave.*' She said it plain."

"But when she said that, maybe she didn't know how long she'd be gone," Kirsten suggested.

"Oh, yes, she knew," Ezra said. He hugged himself as though a shiver went through him.

Kirsten's heart began to beat fast. Surely something awful had happened for Ezra's mother to have left him here like this. Maybe his mother was lost or hurt. Maybe even now she was wandering in the forest or lying in a ravine with a broken leg. "Shouldn't we get everyone to search for your mama?" Kirsten asked.

Ezra shook his head violently. "No! No one should search!"

"But she could be in trouble. We could save her!" Kirsten cried.

"It's too late to save her," he said.

"What do you mean?" Kirsten asked fearfully. "Tell me, *please*."

Ezra took a shuddering breath. "Our

wagon crashed over—you know that. When it crashed, one of the trunks fell on Ma. Her chest was crushed. She grabbed onto my hand. 'Don't leave,' she said. 'I won't leave you, Ma!' I said. 'I promise I won't leave!' She stopped breathing. After a while she got blue and cold." As Ezra spoke, his eyes filled with tears. "She was dead. I buried her." He nodded toward the pile of stones where the black dog sat, its gaze on Ezra as if it understood every word.

"Oh, your poor mama!" Kirsten said. "And poor you, Ezra!" She stepped toward him and reached to touch his shoulder, but he jerked away.

"My last words to Ma were 'I promise I won't leave,'" Ezra repeated. He

Kirsten stepped toward him and reached to touch his shoulder.

scrubbed at his eyes with his fists. "And I won't break my promise, no matter what."

How terrible that his mama had died, that he had been the one to bury her under the pile of stones, that he was left alone. All alone! "You *have* to come home with me, Ezra," Kirsten pleaded.

"No!"

"But last night there was a haze around the moon," Kirsten said. "Papa called it a dog moon. He said a dog moon means bitter cold is coming. You'll freeze out here in the open."

Ezra folded his arms and set his jaw. "I'm sticking to my promise, and you better stick to yours. Don't tell! Now leave me be!" He turned his back on her

and crawled underneath the canvas
wagon top again.

Kirsten trudged back up the road, but
instead of going to school she stood still,
thinking hard. What should she do? Ezra
could die of cold. Wolves could get him.
Ezra needed help badly. And she was the
only one who knew he was here. She had
promised not to tell, but surely this was a
time when "a person is more important
than a promise," as Lars had said. Papa
would know the best thing to do—he
always did. Kirsten turned toward home
and began to run.

♥

In a short while Papa was striding

ahead of Kirsten across the clearing. The black dog barked fiercely, and Ezra came from under the canvas, the rifle at his shoulder. Papa held up his hand. "It's all right," he said in his deep voice. "Put down your gun, boy. I've come to have a word with you, that's all."

Ezra looked at Kirsten angrily. "You promised you wouldn't tell!"

"But I *had* to tell," Kirsten said quickly. "Just let Papa talk to you. Just for a minute."

Ezra lowered the rifle. "Talk then." But he pressed his lips together as if nothing Papa could say would make any difference.

Papa went close to Ezra and crouched down so that his head was on a level with the boy's. "You're a very brave boy. Not many boys would be able to do what you've done for your mama."

Ezra scuffed at the rocks with his worn boot.

"When you get to California, your papa's going to tell you how proud he is of you," Papa went on.

"I'm not going to California. If she told you that, she's wrong," Ezra said, pointing to Kirsten.

"I know you're brave enough to stay here," Papa said, "but I don't think that's what your mama was asking you to do. I think she was asking you to stay until you'd done all you could for her. You have done all you could—all *anyone* could do. The only thing left is to make a marker

for her grave, and I can help
you do that. And then I can take
you to Red Wing."

Ezra frowned and shook his
head.

"Your mama would want you to go to
your friends there, Ezra," Papa insisted.

Ezra bit his lip. Kirsten saw that he
might cry again and that he was desperate
not to. "Are you sure that's what she'd
want?" he asked.

"I'm sure of it," Papa said. "She'd want
you to join your papa. You can trust me on
that. Come along now. I'll hitch up our
wagon, and we'll come pick up your
belongings."

Still Ezra hesitated. "What about Pal?"

he said, nodding toward the dog. "He's guarding Ma. He won't leave. I can't go without him."

Kirsten went to the smashed trunk and lifted out a checkered dress. "Maybe if your dog smelled your mama's clothes, he'd follow the scent," she said.

Ezra looked doubtful, but he took the dress and held it under the dog's nose. The dog snuffled the cotton and whined. Then his tail began to wag. Ezra put his arm around the dog's neck. "Come on, Pal," Ezra said softly. "You've done all you could for Ma. Now we've got to go on our way." Sniffing the dress, the dog followed Ezra from the grave to where Papa and Kirsten waited.

Papa picked up Ezra's rifle, tucked it under his arm, and put his hand on Ezra's shoulder. "We need to get some warm food into you, boy. And I'm sure your horse needs hay."

"Could you feed my dog, too?" Ezra asked. "Pal hasn't eaten hardly anything for days."

"We'll give your dog a good meal!" Kirsten exclaimed. She felt so light with relief that she thought she might float over the trees like a cloud. "I've never seen a dog as loyal as yours, Ezra," she added. "Have you ever known such a loyal dog, Papa?"

"No, I haven't," Papa said. "And I've never known a boy so young to have such a strong heart." He squeezed Kirsten's shoulder. "And I've never known a girl to make a better choice than you did today," he added as they started across the clearing for home.

JANET SHAW

At 8   Now

When I was a young girl, my family often visited a pioneer village museum. One day, my dad helped me climb into a canvas-topped wagon. I wondered how wagons so small could have carried settlers and all their belongings to the West. I imagined Ezra sitting in that wagon when I wrote this story.

Janet Shaw is the author of the Kirsten and Kaya books in The American Girls Collection.

LOOKING
BACK
1854

A PEEK INTO
THE PAST

WAGON TRAINS IN 1854

Ezra and his mother were planning to join other pioneers moving west in a *wagon train*, a long line of covered wagons that traveled together for protection. During Kirsten's time, thousands of pioneers headed to the Oregon and California territories to claim free land or to mine for gold or silver. The 2,000-mile journey took about six months and was not easy, but it was a great adventure—especially for children.

Girls and boys traveling in wagon trains saw many things they had never seen before. The Oregon Trail, the

Herds of buffalo roamed the prairie.

most popular route west, crossed wide rivers, grassy prairies, dry deserts, and the rugged Rocky Mountains. The scenery was beautiful, and children were thrilled to spot quick-footed antelope and large herds of buffalo.

Children also thought it was great fun to eat and sleep

Wagons were freshly painted at the start of the journey.

outdoors. One girl recalled that "every day was like a picnic." In the evenings, the wagons formed a *corral,* or large circle. Safely inside, family members cooked supper—often buffalo or antelope meat—over a fire, then told stories or played the fiddle, sang, and danced. Afterward, children fell asleep in tents or in the backs of the wagons.

Of course, the constant "picnic" had its drawbacks. Cooking over an open fire meant that food was often burned or smelled like ashes. And when it rained,

A wagon train circles for the evening.

fires were hard to build. In the summer, the mosquitoes were so thick that women couldn't keep them out of the bread dough, so most loaves were speckled with bugs! Children complained, too, about the dried apples that were part of their daily diet. Fresh fruits didn't survive the long journey west, so dried apples were usually the only fruit available.

Another drawback to wagon-train life was the hard physical labor. All but the smallest children walked 10 to 15 miles per day because the wagons were full and heavy. While walking, some boys herded cows and horses at the back of the wagon train. Boys also hunted and fished in the evenings. Those whose fathers had traveled west ahead of the wagon train had extra responsibilities, like driving wagons and standing watch at night.

Girls cooked and sewed, cared for babies and the sick, fetched water, and gathered herbs. But some girls also helped with the chores usually reserved for boys, such as herding animals or driving wagons. One 13-year-old girl even joined her father and other men on buffalo hunts!

Cooking over a campfire was more fun in 1907, when dresses weren't required.

Both boys and girls found ways to make games out of their chores, such as when they gathered buffalo dung, or "buffalo chips," to use as fuel for campfires. Children competed against one another to see who could gather the most chips, then stood guard over their family's pile to make sure that it wasn't raided!

For many years, families that settled in the West relied on cow dung for fuel.

Children found other creative ways to pass the time. They chanted rhymes or sang rounds. They gathered wildflowers to weave into wreaths or necklaces. They played tag and hide-and-seek in the tall prairie grass and other games that children still play today, such as London Bridge and leapfrog. Children also made up stories, many of which featured Indians and expressed the fear some pioneers had of Indian attacks and kidnappings.

Children sang songs we sing today, like "Oh! Susanna."

Some Indians living on the Great Plains served as guides for pioneers.

In fact, attacks by Indians were rare in the early 1850s. Most Indians helped the pioneers by giving them fresh meat, fish, and berries in exchange for cloth, iron pans, and tools. But as more pioneers traveled west—claiming land, hunting buffalo, and bringing diseases—some tribes tried to fight back. By the 1860s, warfare with Indians was more common.

Children in the 1850s faced greater danger in the form of illness. Diseases such as measles, smallpox, and typhoid swept through the wagon trains. Cholera, the most deadly, spread because of unclean conditions and dirty drinking water. Some children were orphaned when both parents died from a disease. Like Ezra, these children had to take on adult responsibilities at an early age.

Pioneers fought illness with tonics from doctors and with homemade remedies found in recipe books.

Accidents, too, were common on the trail. Many children were injured or even killed when they fell or leaped off wagons and were caught beneath the wheels. Some children died during river crossings, in animal stampedes, or when they wandered away from camp and got lost.

About one in twenty people travel-ing west died during the journey. The dead were buried beside the trail, their graves a constant reminder to others that death could strike at any time. Many graves

Graves were marked by wooden crosses or carved stones.

belonged to children. One stone read, "Rest in peace, sweet boy, for thy travels are over." The boy was 12 years old.

In spite of the dangers, most children traveling in wagon trains kept their spirits up. When they reached the trail's end, they were strong and ready to help their parents build a home in the new territory. But they would never forget the giant "picnic" along the trail that had led them there.

Children helped fill the cracks in their new log homes with mud.

MAKE A FLOWER CROWN
Pretend that you're traveling the trail!

Children traveling in wagon trains passed through prairies covered with wildflowers. Girls spent hours gathering the flowers and weaving them into chains of different shapes and sizes. They made wreaths, necklaces, and crowns out of the fresh flowers.

Gather some flowers of your own, and make a flower crown that's just your size.

YOU WILL NEED:

An adult to help you

*20 to 25 daisies or other flowers
with sturdy stems*

Scissors

Cutting board

Small knife

Large paper clip

*3 to 6 pieces of ribbon,
18 inches long*

1. Use the scissors to trim the stems of the flowers to 3 inches.

2. Have an adult help you make a slit through the middle of each stem. Lay the flower on a cutting board, and push the tip of the knife through the middle of the stem.

3. Pass a flower stem through the slit in another. Be sure to pull the second stem all the way through the first.

4. Keep passing flower stems through one another until you have a chain long enough to go around your head.

5. Use the paper clip to join the stem of the last flower to the stem of the first flower. Tie the ribbons around the stems just beside the paper clip, and remove the paper clip.

American Girl ®

PO BOX 620497
MIDDLETON WI 53562-0497

American Girl ®

Catalogue Request

Join our mailing list! Just drop this card
in the mail, call **1-800-845-0005**, or visit
our Web site at **americangirl.com.**

Send me a catalogue:

Name
_____

Address
_____

City _____ State ___ Zip 1961i

Girl's birth date: ___/___/___
month day year

Parent's signature
_____

Send my friend a catalogue:

Name
_____

Address
_____

City _____ State ___ Zip 1225i

E-mail
_____